Gawain Greytail

and the Terrible Tab

For Lucan, my Second Assistant – C.F.

To Valeria and Daniel – M.A.

Published in 2021 in Great Britain by
Barrington Stoke Ltd
18 Walker Street, Edinburgh, EH3 7LP

www.barringtonstoke.co.uk

This edition based on *Gawain Greytail and the Terrible Tab*
(Barrington Stoke, 2015)

This story was originally published in a different
form in a German edition: "Gawain von Grauschwanz
und die schreckliche Meg" (extract from: *Leselöwen –
Rittergeschichten*) © 1994 Loewe Verlag GmbH, Bindlach

Translation © 2015 & 2021 Barrington Stoke
Illustrations © 2015 Mónica Armiño

A CIP catalogue record for this book is available
from the British Library upon request

ISBN: 978-1-80090-077-6

Printed by Hussar Books, Poland

Barrington Stoke

Gawain Greytail

and the Terrible Tab

Cornelia Funke

Illustrated by
Mónica Armiño

Rook Castle was full of happy mice.
Castle mice.

But Sir Tristan, the lord of Rook Castle, was cross. His chain mail was all chewed up. There were mouse droppings everywhere.

So Sir Tristan bought a cat called Tab – the best mouse catcher in the land.

Tab got to work. Soon only three mice were left – Shuffle, Snuffle and Scuffle. They were starving and scared.

"We need a new home!" Shuffle said.

"But where?" Scuffle cried. "We are castle mice. There are no other castles nearby."

Things were very bad.

But the next night, someone new scurried into the castle. He wore a tiny suit of armour that shone in the light of the moon.

It was the famous mouse knight Gawain Greytail. Every cat in the land was scared of him.

"First, we need to get you some armour and three big sharp needles," Gawain said.

"I can get needles," Scuffle whispered. "But where will we get armour?"

"We can make it from bits of metal," Gawain
said. "Now, let's get to work!"

And when Tab came to stop them, brave
Gawain led her away.

When the armour was finished, it was not as splendid as Gawain's, but it would keep the three mice safe from Tab's sharp claws.

"Now take the needles," Gawain said, "and let's chase Tab away for ever."

So the mice tiptoed through the dark castle.

Terrible Tab lay in front of the fire.
When the four mice ran towards her,
she jumped up.

"Helloooo!" she purred. "Yum. Dinner."

"Cower and shiver, Terrible Tab!" Gawain cried. "I am Gawain Greytail and these are my three brave knights. Now, clear off!"

Tab laughed, then jumped at Gawain.

Gawain stepped to one side and Tab landed on her nose. She hissed and clawed at the mice, but their armour kept them safe.

"Clear off, Tab!" Scuffle shouted. He poked Tab with his needle.

"Yes, get lost!" Shuffle waved his needle under Tab's nose.

"We were here first!" Snuffle cried. He chopped off one of Tab's whiskers.

Tab stepped back. She had never seen anything like this. Why didn't the mice just run away? Why weren't they afraid?

"Get lost!" the mice cried. "Look! We've opened the window for you."

Gawain jumped onto Tab's head. "Tell
all your cat friends about the mice of
Rook Castle," he hissed. And he bit Tab
on the ear.

"Meooooow!" Tab cried.

She leapt out of the window and vanished into the dark night.

The four mice slammed the window shut.

23

The next morning, Sir Tristan couldn't find Tab anywhere.

Soon the castle was full of mouse droppings again. And so Sir Tristan bought another cat – then another, and another. None of the cats stayed for long.

In the end, the family tried mouse traps.

But all that they ever trapped was forks and needles.

HAVE YOU READ THEM ALL?

ACORNS growing readers

Pancake Face
Georgia Byng
Illustrated by Mike Phillips

Freddy and the PIG
Charlie Higson
Illustrated by Mark Chambers

Teresa Flavin
YELLOW Rabbit
Illustrated by Rich Watson

Harry and Kate at the Book Museum
Sophie McKenzie
ILLUSTRATED BY MARTIN REMPHRY

Catherine MacPhail
JENNY'S choice
Illustrated by Vladimir Stankovic

Michael Morpurgo
All I Said Was ...
Illustrated by Ross Collins

Cornelia Funke

Gawain Greytail and the Terrible Tab

Illustrated by Monica Armino

MOLLY ROGERS

PIRATE GIRL

Cornelia Funke

Illustrated by Kasia Matyjaszek

ALEXANDER McCALL SMITH

BOING BOING

ILLUSTRATED BY ZOE PERSICO

Michael Rosen

Illustrated by Richard Watson

MAD IN THE BACK

MICHAEL ROSEN

Wolfman

Illustrated by Chris Mould

ELEANOR UPDALE

Illustrated by Sarah Horne

Itch Scritch Scratch